STEP INTO READING®

3
STEP
READING ON YOUR OWN

P9-CNB-595

☆ American Girl®

Molly's
Christmas Surprise

by Lauren Clauss

illustrated by Melissa Manwill

Random House 🏠 New York

Meet Molly McIntire!

Molly is a nine-year-old girl who

lives in a small town in 1944.

She is fun, friendly,

and patriotic.

Molly has two brothers

and a sister.

Molly's dad is a doctor
for the army. The United States
is fighting in World War II,
so Dad is in England
taking care of wounded soldiers.

Molly's mom helps with
the war effort at home.
Mom volunteers for the Red Cross.
She also takes care
of the family.

Molly's sister, Jill,
is fourteen
and loves fashion.

Her brother Ricky
is twelve.
He likes to tease.

And Brad is five.

Despite the war, Molly's life
has stayed mostly the same.
She still goes to school
and plays with her friends.
She loves to tap-dance!

But Molly's life has changed
because of the war, too.
Her family—just like every family
in America—has to ration food.
This means they are only allowed
to buy a certain amount
of some foods.

Molly's family grows vegetables
in their backyard.
This way, they don't have to buy
all their food.

Molly is excited for Christmas!
She wonders if Dad will send
any presents from England.
She writes a letter to ask him.

Jill tells Molly
that they may not hear
from their dad.
He is very busy.

Molly knows Jill is right, but
she can't help hoping Dad will
send something. In her letter,
Molly told Dad that she wanted
a doll for Christmas. That night,
Molly's mom talks to her.

She tells Molly it's never wrong
to hope for good things,
especially at Christmastime.
"Christmas will be different this
year," Mom says. "We'll just
have to make our own surprises!"

The next morning, Molly, Ricky, and Jill get out the Christmas decorations. They are excited to decorate the tree.

But they have to get the tree first!

Since Dad is away

and Mom is shopping with Brad,

the kids combine their money

to buy the tree themselves.

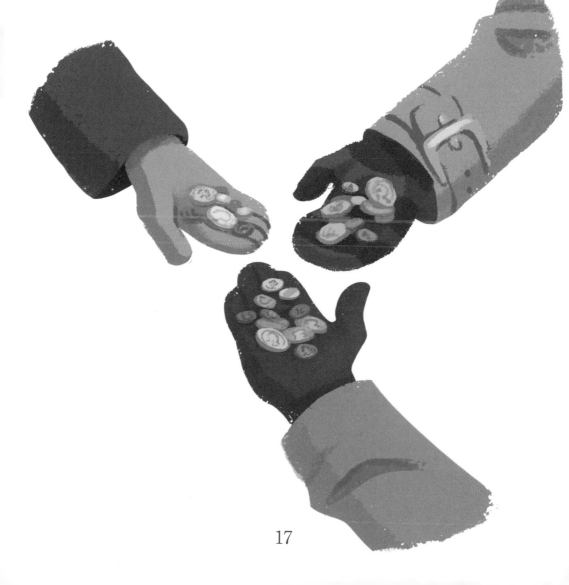

"This is it," Jill says, pointing
to a small, skinny tree.
It's not as pretty and full
as the other trees,
but it costs less.
The piney Christmas smell
cheers Molly up.

CHRISTMAS TREES

"Let's decorate the tree
to surprise Mom and Brad
when they get home!" says Molly.
Once the ornaments and tinsel
are hung, the tree doesn't look
scrawny—it looks beautiful!

The next morning, Molly wakes up
and sees that it has snowed.
Now it really feels like Christmas!
Molly runs outside in her
pajamas to play in the snow.

Ricky opens his window.

He gathers some snow and throws

a snowball at Molly! She laughs.

Jill joins Molly outside,

and the sisters make snow angels

and build snowmen all morning.

At lunchtime, Molly and Jill
head inside. By the front door,
they see a snow-covered package.
It's from Dad! The box says
"Keep Hidden Until Christmas."

"Let's hide it in the garage,"
Molly says.

Molly and Jill take the box
into the garage and cover it
with a blanket.

But keeping the box a secret
is hard!
Over the next few days,
Molly makes sure no one
gets too close to it.

Molly is relieved when they
go to the Christmas Eve service.
The secret is safe while everyone
is at church.

Later that night, after everyone
else has gone to bed,
Molly and Jill sneak into
the garage and get the box. They
quietly put it under the tree.

The next morning, everyone is delighted to see the box from Dad! Molly and Jill share a smile and tell the family about the secret. Everyone is glad that the girls saved the box for a special Christmas-morning treat.

The family opens the box,

and everyone gets a present!

Jill gets a new hat.

Ricky gets a silk pilot scarf.

Brad gets a soldier helmet.

Mom gets leather gloves.

And Molly gets a doll
dressed as a nurse.
It is exactly what they each
wanted! At the bottom of the box
is a note telling them
to turn on the radio.

Mom turns on the radio.
The station is playing messages
from servicemen in England.
The family hears
a familiar voice.

It is Dad!

"I'd like to say merry Christmas
to the merry McIntires,"
he says. The family is so happy.
Hearing Dad's voice
is the best gift of all!

When the broadcast is over,
the family starts making
a big Christmas breakfast.
Molly hugs her nurse doll tight.
She is so thankful—even though
her dad is far away, he was
with them on Christmas after all!